I0786943

# ILLUMI-NAUGHTY

## A Conspiracy Club's Unfortunate Mishap

## BRIAN C HAILES

# INITIATION

I had never joined a club before but having just moved from the Midwest to the quiet town of New Haven, Connecticut, I would do about anything to make friends. Particularly on the second week of the new school year. So, I determined that I would get to know the first person to sit next to me at lunch. As it turned out, that was Kennedy.

"Hey, do you mind?" he asked, sitting even before I could nod my permission. Tall, outspoken, and animated in his movements, he made me feel welcome, at ease, and instantly brought me into his tight-knit group of 'conspiracy theorist' friends, always elaborating on the latest bit of news and how it fit into this elitist scheme or that historic religious philosophy. I must admit, I was intrigued at first—especially when he pulled me backstage behind the curtains after school got out on a Tuesday—but I had no idea how far down the rabbit hole it would take us.

I guess that made me *Alice*.

"What's up everybody?" Kennedy said, patting me on the back in front of five of his fellow Conspiracy Club members. "This here's Ciman, with a "C." He's new to our school, and I thought we could show him around a bit, see if he's possibly interested in initiation. He says he loves conspiracies, while he doesn't often believe in them."

"Yeah," I said, "but I do find them fascinating—"

"What makes you think he's worthy?" the dapper kid with glasses standing in the back asked Kennedy. "Have you put him through a vetting process?"

*"Worthy?"* I asked, trying to decide if he was serious or not. "Is he joking?"

"Don't worry," said Kennedy, "We'll get to that one."

"Hi Ciman," said the blonde girl in front. "I'm Dotty, but you can call me Redrum."

*"Redrum?"* I asked.

"Yeah," said Kennedy. "Murder spelled backwards, you know, from—"

"I know what it's from," I said.

A shallow sense of relief washed over all gathered.

Kennedy pointed at the curly-haired ginger in a striped sweater, standing off to one side. "That's Murphy. He wants to be a lawyer. Get it?"

"Murphy's Law," I muttered. "Nice."

"We don't all use our real names here in the club," said Kennedy. "It's, like, our thing."

"His name's not even Kennedy." Redrum giggled. "It's Roy, Roy Charlotte Stinger."

He glared at her, then looked over at me.

"I didn't know that." I grinned.

He didn't grin back. "Kennedy will be fine."

"He doesn't like 'Roy,'" Redrum mouthed. "Or 'Charlotte.'"

"Got it," I said. "'Kennedy,' after the . . . *JFK assassination*, I assume?"

"Don't get him started," said the dark-haired kid next to Murphy.

"That's Gabe," said Kennedy. "He's the most religious of the group. Goes to Bible study every morning . . . *early*. He brings some good insights from time to time."

"Oh, as in *Gabriel?*" I asked.

Gabe nodded. "Or *Noah* for short. Good to meet you, Ciman. The real question is do you believe in a *pre*-tribulation rapture or a *post*-tribulation rapture?"

"I'm not sure I even know what that means," I said, shaking my head.

He smiled. "Neither do these jokers."

"The kid that doesn't think you're worthy," Kennedy said, "We call him Adam."

"As in 'Adam and Eve'?" I asked.

"No," Adam said, "Adam Weishaupt, the German law professor who pushed Enlightenment ideals. My real name's Jack Lowe. And I still don't think you're worthy."

"Gotcha," I said, wondering what I'd done to offend him. "Nice to meet you."

"If you are going to join our club," Kennedy said, "there are a few things you need to know."

"First," said Redrum, "*All* conspiracy theories have a few certain necessary elements: A plot between two or more people, a secret action, and a motive. But the ones that take off usually have a little something extra."

Kennedy piped in. "The successful ones confirm what people *want* to believe."

"Interest and excitement in offering 'big' explanations for 'big' events helps too," said Murphy. "But we're more interested in the truth. Not your 'individual truth' or 'truth born of social contagion,' but real, unmistakable, *universal truth*."

"We like to call it the 'solid'," said Kennedy.

"Conspiracy theorists are simply people who see the truth before everyone else," Gabe added.

"Right," I said. "Okay. I agree. True or false, black, white, right and wrong. I'm with you."

"Don't misunderstand," said Kennedy, "There can be a lot of gray area in the world, I mean, look around: money, politics, celebrity, influence, . . . relationships can get messy. Stories can easily get covered up or be manipulated. Even made up completely. Different agendas vying for attention, the propaganda machines working overtime to send a cocktail of dangerous messages. And don't even get me started on A.I. Our job here is research. Real, honest research."

"Sure, yeah," I said. "That makes sense . . . for a club about . . . consp—"

"Oh yeah," said Adam, sarcastically. "I'd say he's ripe for initiation."

"Ignore him," said Kennedy. "I know it sounds boring, but I haven't told you what we're currently researching."

"No? What's that? Skull and Bones?" I asked, proud to think up and display my limited knowledge that a widespread conspiracy took place right down the street.

"Maybe that's a part of it," Kennedy said playfully. "Drum roll, Gabe."

Gabe flipped his backpack around and mock drummed on it with his hands.

"Wait for it," said Redrum. "*Wait for it . . .*"

"The Ancient and Illuminated Seers of Bavaria," Murphy announced.

I shook my head, confused.

"The Illumi-freakin'-nati," Kennedy clarified.

"Oh, yeah," I said. "That's a popular one."

"Likely *the* most popular one," Gabe said, "As secret societies go."

"That's debatable," Adam cut in. "The biggest conspiracy theory of all is that the government cares about you and exists to serve the citizens."

I offered a courtesy chuckle. Apparently, the others had heard that one before.

"Or the scariest explanation of all . . ." he continued, nonplussed. ". . . That there is no evil plot, conspiracy, or corruption, and our government is genuinely unintelligent."

I chuckled again, for real this time.

"Don't stop," Redrum said to Adam. "By all means, keep going. You're on a roll. Maybe you could pull one out we haven't all heard a million times or read in a meme."

"Sure. What if Harry Potter never went to Hogwarts . . . and created a false reality to cope with living under the stairs?"

She tilted her head to one side. "That one's not bad."

"Okay, now I'm good," he said with a wink, to which she rolled her eyes, and checked her phone.

"All right then," Kennedy said, like a natural born leader, taking charge. "Are we gonna do this?!"

Adam shook his head. Everyone else looked at me and smiled.

"The smiles have it." Kennedy walked over and grabbed a dusty chair from behind a black curtain and dragged it to center stage. "Have a seat, my man."

I took a reluctant step forward and did as I was told, my anxiety rising. "Repeat after me," Kennedy said, holding his arm to the square. "I, Ciman—what's your last name?"

"Humphrey."

"I, Ciman Humphrey, solemnly swear to remain curious, and to study diligently the actual evidence of a case or 'alleged' case like a non-biased investigative journalist, taking all 'fake news' with a grain of salt, and to get to the bottom of any and all conspiracies brought before this consecrated club of open-minded individuals based on proof alone (and sometimes, the unmistakable writing on the wall).”

“I have to repeat all that?” I said, my brain scrambling. “Do you have it written down somewhere?”

“Just raise your hand and say you agree,” said Redrum.

“I agree.” I hesitantly raised my hand.

“Woo-hoo,” Adam said in a mocking tone, which everyone ignored. “The Oddball Assembly has one more.”

“Good enough,” said Redrum, glancing up from her phone.

“Welcome to the Conspiracy Club,” Kennedy said, as everyone patted me on the back—except Adam. “Oh, and we do have two other members who weren’t able to be here: Rosi and Mason.

“Those their *real* names?” I asked.

“He’s catching on,” said Gabe, as he re-secured his backpack over his shoulders.

“That’s right,” Murphy added. “Question everything.”

“Rosi (after the Rosicrucians),” Kennedy said, “And Mason—”

“Freemasons.” I clasped Kennedy’s outstretched hand, and he pulled me to my feet.

“Let’s get to work,” he said.

I nodded. “Sounds good . . . uh . . . *What are we doing again?*”

# THE MEETING

 $W$ alking down into Gabe's basement, the club's supposed 'headquarters', I half expected to find a chaotic mess of newspaper clippings, red strings connecting seemingly unrelated events, and a chalkboard covered in cryptic symbols. Yet, surprisingly, none of those things were present.

"I feel like we should be playing Dungeons and Dragons or something," I joked as we all gathered around a small table and took a seat.

"What do you mean?" Kennedy asked.

I leaned forward over the card table in the center of the dimly lit basement. "I dunno, it's Friday night, we're gathered down here like D&D nerds talking conspiracies . . ."

They all gazed back at me with raised eyebrows.

"None of you have ever played RPGs before? Really?"

Dead stares.

"I have to say, that surprises me—Never mind."

Kennedy jumped in to rescue me from the conversation, and Redrum leaned over to whisper in my ear. "I've played D&D with my older brothers. *I* know what you're talking about. But then, I am the enigmatic artist with a penchant for drawing conspiratorial doodles in the margins of my notebooks."

"Thank you," I whispered. "I'd like to see those sometime."

She grinned, before returning her attention across the table.

"So, how many of you have been to the Peabody Museum?" Kennedy asked.

Everyone raised their hands except me.

"By the way," Kennedy said, "Mason, this is our newest member,

Ciman, with a "C," initiated the other day while you were, what, at the dentist?"

"Orthodontist." Mason nodded warmly, displaying his braces. "Nice to meet you, Ciman. Rosi, my sister, couldn't be here tonight either, but she does look forward to meeting you sometime. She plays, like, three sports, and is on the debate team. She's an overachiever."

"Gotcha," I said, and we shook hands, which felt awkward with everyone watching. "Half expected you to use a secret handshake."
That warranted a few titters from the club.

"Not until you make it to the *eighth* level of Scientology," Mason said with a serious tone, tightening his grip, to which, I didn't know what to say.

"Kidding." He laughed.

"Adam," Kennedy said, "Why don't you bring Ciman up to speed on the basics, and then, Mason, you can give us a rundown of the museums we talked about, and their significance to the group project for Mrs. Orwell—she's the one that signed off on our club, so we report to her on our activities from time to time."

Adam pursed his lips and let out a long sigh as he stood. Only now did I notice how much taller he was than everyone else in the room. "So," he began with a shrug, "we've investigated the existence and alleged activities of the Illuminati for some time. Most of us have read the books, and we all understand there's an overwhelming amount of conspiracy theories, hidden history, half-truths, and hoaxes surrounding the group. We know the original Bavarian society, formed in the eighteenth century, opposed superstition, religious influence, and state authority. But did they die off? Or did they carry on becoming the shadowy elite who control the world? I mean, what is their *real* history, and do they still exist today? That's what we intend to find out. Right? Good? Am I done?"

I glanced around at everyone and raised my hand.

"New guy," Adam said, pointing at me.

"Um, yeah," I said. "*How* exactly? Haven't people been trying to expose their secrets for decades? *Centuries* even?"

Adam looked at Kennedy, and Kennedy looked at me. "Yes. We'll get to that. First, Gabe's also got some important insights to bring everyone up to speed on—from his Bible studies, I guess? Gabe?"

"Sure, yeah, okay." Gabe stood up nervously as Adam took his seat. "So, ask yourself this: What if the government is behind *stupid* conspiracy theories to make the *real* ones less obvious?"

"Like Satan using songs played backwards to control your mind?" Redrum asked with a grin.

"Good one," I whispered to her.

"Yeah," Gabe said. "Exactly." He cleared his throat. "Um, I know Adam mentioned Weishaupt and the original Bavarian crew as being opposed to religious influence but consider this . . . Oh, and then there was also the discordianism and those two Playboy guys that published that popular trilogy that gathered steam in the 60s and 70s. And that ended up pushing all the speculation of 'Illuminatus' into the realm of the hokey but . . . hear me out for a second. There are some well-known Bible prophecies that talk about an evil lady rising in the last days."

"I think her name is 'Karen'," Kennedy said, tongue-in-cheek.

"Yeah," Gabe said. "I like that. Probably. Anyway, she's the *'Propaganda Minister'*. The seductive courtesan who rides the beast, her mount, which is described as a lamb with two horns—by John, the Revelator."

"Sorry," I said, interrupting, "But that sounds a little hokey to me."

"I think it sounds pretty cool," said Redrum.

And that was enough to shut me up.

"Anyway," Gabe said, "In my class on the Book of Revelation last year, I learned what she was all about: She promises a person they can do whatever they want and get away with it. Sound familiar? Now, the *beast*, her organization, provides the muscle—makes it all possible. Like Babylon of old, her organization is the accumulation of *worldly* powers. The earthly counterpart of Hell."

"So, what are you talking about here?" Kennedy asked. "More recent societies—Commission on Foreign Relations? Trilateral Commission? Bilderbergers?"

Gabe tilted his head to one side. "Perhaps."

"Okay," I said. "I'll admit, that does sound pretty cool, but what does it have to do with proving the Illuminati still exists?"

"Maybe nothing," he said, nonchalantly. And then he leaned forward for effect, "Or maybe . . . *EVERYTHING.*"

"So, you're saying the evil lady Karen's organization and the secret society we're researching are one and the same?" I folded my arms, leaning back in my chair, surprised to find myself playing the skeptic. But how could I not?

"I'm only saying it's possible," Gabe raised his hands innocently.

"Fair enough," Kennedy said. "And thanks, Gabe. We like to keep an open mind, consider all avenues. It's all part of the oath, after all. We're not tying string around anyone's genitals, forcing them to drink blood or making anyone jack off in a coffin while spilling their darkest secrets—"

"*What?!*" I exclaimed.

"Oh," Kennedy said, clearly realizing he dropped insights far beyond my shallow pool of knowledge on the topic. "Sorry, Ciman. I take it you haven't read the old Frenchman's account of the Illuminati's initiation process? Or Skull and Bones?"

I shook my head. "Uh-uh."

"Well, we'll get you up to speed," he said. "Murphy? You look deep in thought. What's up?"

*"I think I've seen Gabe's 'Propaganda Minister',"* said Murphy.

We all took a moment to digest the comment.

"In person?" Kennedy as ked to which Murphy nodded.

"I think so," he said. "She works at the Peabody Museum."

"How could you possibly know that?" I asked.

"I didn't claim to *know*," Murphy said timidly, "but I've been researching this stuff for a long time. As I see it, the globalists' plan has been to squeeze America into a globalist society by positioning China and America into a continuation of the next Cold War, which would lead to a worldwide technocracy. 'New World Order' is all about technocracy, complete control not only of technology and financial markets, but of people's biology."

"What does that have to do with the local museum?" Kennedy asked. "The Skull and Bones, specifically G. Stanley Hall, played a significant role in importing the Prussian education system to America, right? Shaping the country's educational landscape to support such an order?"

"Okay, sure," Kennedy said. "He helped to lay the foundation work. I follow."

*I didn't.*

Murphy continued, "Right. Well, public education systems were designed by the same oligarchical forces to keep people unaware of their origins and the true power structures in society. The influence and control exerted by Skull and Bones on the education side and Illuminati on the world's power stage through this system is difficult to detect, as it operates through social engineering."

"Isn't that why Disney is hosing its shareholders?" Adam asked. "Because social engineering has become more important to the billionaires than turning an immediate profit?"

"Short answer?" Kennedy said. "Yes. But we digress."

"So ..." Redrum said, "Again, what does all of this have to do with the Natural History Museum across town?"

Murphy held up both hands, then dropped them. "G. Stanley Hall—the psychologist and educator from the early twentieth century with famously eugenic views—well, he has a granddaughter, Ingrid Stanley Ahlgren, who happens to work at the Peabody Museum. Actually, she directs it; she's the museum curator."

"And you think she is Gabe's *'Propaganda Minister'?*" Mason asked, skeptical. "That title could apply to a whole slew of people—alive or dead—or even an entire system."

Avoiding eye contact with Mason, as was his manner with everyone, Murphy simply nodded. "You're not wrong, but I'll show you my research—I'm almost certain of it. Although she is most certainly not acting alone." He shook his head. "Not even close."

# THE PROPANGANDA MINISTER

"Man walks into a bar," Gabe said, "orders a Corona and two Hurricanes . . . Bartender says, that'll be $20.20."

No one laughed.

"Get it?" Gabe asked. "2020?"

"Got it," I said. "That's good. Now, why can't we walk through the front doors again?"

"That would be suspicious," said Redrum. "Large groups of teenagers don't wander into museums on their own without being forced by parents or on a field trip with the school."

"And lurking behind bushes across the street from this museum isn't suspicious at all."

"The CCTV street cams don't reach this far," said Mason.

"Okay," I said. "So, what's the plan?"

"Reconnaissance," Kennedy said. "We'll scout out the place. See what we can see. Murphy, you got your etching paper?"

"Yeah," he answered, tapping his pocket.

*Etching paper?* I thought, curious, but not enough to ask.

Not that I minded galivanting across New Haven with this newfound group of eccentric misfits. Connecticut held a certain historic charm and cultural richness, and the newly renovated Peabody Museum, nestled amid a collection of other nicely refurbished buildings, seemed no different, even from across the busy street. And although they were a peculiar group of high school students that defied conventional social norms, I embraced the unlikely friendship.

"I mean, I guess we could be cruising chicks at the mall."

"There's always time for that," Kennedy said with a smirk.

From the look on her face, Redrum didn't appreciate where the conversation was headed, and changed the subject. "Let's split up and walk inside next to groups already entering. Then we'll reconnect once inside and case the place."

"Good plan," Kennedy said. "I'll go first."

One-by-one, they took off and entered the museum with other visitors, a few of which gave them strange looks if they walked too close or ran up too enthusiastically to hold open the door.

Now it was my turn, so I quickly jaywalked across the street to make my approach. However, the only other nearby patrons closing in on the front entry were an African American lady with her two young kids. But I'd already committed. Besides, she very well could have adopted a platinum blonde, white boy ten years older than her next youngest. *Perfectly feasible,* I thought, until I saw the looks from the club members inside, and the confused and protective reaction of the nice mother as she whisked her kids away from me upon entering.

The club may have been united by their love for conspiracy theories, mysterious occurrences, and the thrill of the unknown, but I had a lot to learn if I was to become a contributing member of the group. I also had the nagging feeling that Kennedy, Redrum, and the others would soon thrust me into the heart of a perilous . . . *adventure* wasn't the right word . . . *ordeal.*

Redrum gestured sharply for me to join her. "Get over here!" she whispered. Like a good puppy, I obeyed.

"What's the plan?" I asked, also in a low whisper.

"Come on," she said. "Murphy wants to show us something in the Egyptian wing."

"Sounds good."

A hefty security guard, eyeing us suspiciously as we approached, held up a stiff hand to prevent our entering. "Ya'all have a ticket?"

"I thought it was free," I said.

"You'll need to make a donation at the front desk," he answered, pointing behind us.

"A *mandatory* donation? That's kind of an oxymoron—"

Redrum put a gentle hand on my shoulder to shut me up, and she turned to the man. "We need to use the restroom," she said in her high-pitched singsong voice. "If I remember, it's down the hall there. Right?"

He let out a tired sigh. "Go ahead."

And we were in!

We hurried past the restrooms and into the main gallery.

"That was brilliant!" I said as we ran.

"Shhh," she giggled. "*Mandatory* donation. Can you believe it?"

"In today's world? Yeah."

"Follow me," she said, tugging on my arm, and dragging me past a giant collection of dinosaur fossils, looming over one of the great rooms.

"Wow," I said, peering up into the gallery at what remained of the prehistoric beasts.

"Haven't you ever seen dinosaur bones before?" she asked.

"Well, yeah, but—" I didn't want to finish my thought by saying, *"But not with you,"* so I kept quiet.

"I'm still confused," I said at length. "What does a natural history museum next to an Ivy League university like Yale have to do with Skull and Bones, and, by extension, the Illuminati?"

"It's an old school," said Redrum, "Founded in 1701. And it's where the Skull and Bones order originated."

The two passed a massive hanging banner that read: "STRATEGIC PRIORITIES FOR DIVERSITY, EQUITY, ACCESSIBILITY & INCLUSION."

"Yeah," she added. "'Woke' too. There's also the Grove Street Cemetery down the road, dating from the late 18th century, and the Egyptian Revival gateway. Not to mention all the hidden symbols in New Haven's architecture. I don't know if *Grove* Street's got ties to the Bohemian *Grove* out in San Francisco, but in the Conspiracy Club, we don't discount coincidences."

We finally found our way to the 'Echoes of Egypt' exhibition in the far wing of the museum, where Kennedy, Adam, Murphy, Mason, and Gabe all gathered around a roped-off life-size Egyptian sarcophagus covered in ancient hieroglyphics.

Kennedy and Murphy, both with their backs to the closest monitoring ceiling cams, whipped out their phones and snapped a few shots.

"What's significant about this one?" I asked quietly.

Murphy barely acknowledged my presence. "There's a picture of it hanging in Ahlgren's office, front and center."

"Maybe she likes mummies," Adam said. *"And how did you get inside her office?"*

"Came here with my mom and sister and I had her ask for a special tour. Only, the picture hanging in Ahlgren's office didn't have the whole sarcophagus with all the markings, so here we are. Now we do. My uncle's friend is an Egyptologist out west, and I want to send these pictures to him—ask what these symbols are about—I haven't been able to find this particular sarcophagus in any of the books on the subject."

"That's . . . something," I said. "*Thorough.* Still, that doesn't prove the curator is involved in anything nefarious."

"No, but I followed her last week, and she walked straight from the museum to "The Tomb."

"The Tomb?" I asked.

Redrum leaned close to whisper in my ear, "Skull and Bones headquarters. It's where they initiate new members."

"Oh." I somehow felt like I should have known that.

"Wait," Gabe said. "You've been stalking the woman?"

"Well, it paid off, didn't it?"

We all raised our eyebrows, tilted our heads.

"I thought women weren't allowed inside The Tomb," Mason said.

Adam piped in. "That changed a decade ago."

"Why don't we go and join Skull and Bones ourselves?" I asked Kennedy. "You and Adam look like you're old enough to be in college. *Mystery solved.*"

"You've got to be from a family of wealth or political influence," Kennedy answered. "And you've got to be *invited.* Each of the six groups consists of 15 members of the senior class, a total of 90—well less than 10 percent of the class. Every spring, on "tap day," each society elects 15 members among the juniors as their successors."

"Gotcha." I scratched my jaw. "And why is there still so little known about these secret societies?"

"Oh, I dunno," Redrum said sarcastically. "Blackmail, threat of a smeared reputation, torture, death. It's what *'Skull and Bones'* means: *'Death and Danger'.* Like on a pirate's flag."

"Got it."

A large group of museum visitors suddenly entered the room, and we moved along, following the exit signs.

As we emerged into the open lobby, Murphy froze up. "It's *HER!*" he exclaimed in a stifled whisper. "It's Ahlgren."

From across the high-ceilinged room, a well-manicured woman in a form-fitting suit jacket and pencil skirt immediately caught my attention. She carried an intimidating air of professionalism and self-importance. She clutched a digital pad to her chest and spotted us from across the way.

"Shut up," Kennedy whispered. "Just act normal. We're leaving."

As we made for the doors, the dark-haired businesswoman slowly walked forward on her high heels, barring our escape. Flashing an unnaturally white smile, she peered down at us like a condescending preschool teacher. "Why hello there," she said. "I'm Ingrid. Museum curator. You know, we don't get a lot of teenagers coming through. I'm so pleased to see all of you."

Several moments of awkward silence passed between us.

*What could we say? Could this lady actually be involved in the things everyone was talking about? In the real world?*

Her eyes moved over us as if cataloguing our faces one-by-one. She paused at the tall ginger. "You there . . . *Murphy* was it? Did you not visit us the other day?"

*Good memory.*

Petrified, Murphy shyly nodded up at her, while his eyes remained fixed on the floor. "Y-yes, ma'am."

"And polite . . . *Yes*, I remember giving you and your sister a tour—even brought you to my office. What an adorable girl, your sister. And your mother, so gracious."

"Is there something we can do for you?" Kennedy asked, rescuing poor Murphy from her metaphorical talons.

She smiled and turned her gaze upon Kennedy like a mountain lion suddenly contemplating the taste of a young buck. "Anything you can do for me?" she asked, pretending to be flattered. "Why yes. Tell me what you thought of our exhibits, the renovations. You know, it took us *three years . . . Way* longer than expected."

"It's a lovely museum," Kennedy said. "You did a great job. We're all suckers for dinosaurs. Oh, and the murals, amazing—"

"Yes, they're quite famous," she said abruptly. "Tell me, did you find anything of interest in our *Egypt* exhibit?" Again, she glanced back at Murphy.

*Yikes.* I suddenly remembered Redrum's comment about coincidences. "W-we didn't have a lot of time," Redrum said, cutting in. "Our, um, our *parents* are *expecting* us. They'll be here any minute to pick us up. I mean, they're probably here now."

"I see," said the woman. "Well, we wouldn't want to keep them waiting." Her professionally manufactured smile sent a chill up my spine. "Lovely meeting you all," she said. "Do come again."

When she walked off, clearing the path to the doors, we couldn't get outside fast enough, although even outside of the building, I could still feel her cold stare through the glass.

"Is it me or was that—?"

"—*Creepy,*" Redrum said, right as Gabe said, "—*Weird.*"

I glanced at Kennedy. "For a second there, I thought she was going to ask you on a date."

"You can have her," he replied. "She's no 'MILF'."

Redrum giggled, as we made our way down the sidewalk past the trees.

"So, what do we do now?" Gabe asked.

"More research," Kennedy said. "And . . ."

"And what?" Mason asked.

Adam shook his head with a humorless smile. "Don't say it."

Everyone seemed to be in on the unspoken plan except me.

Mason, the second-most clueless of the group, spoke up first. "Are you suggesting we put the 'old lady' under surveillance?"

"We can take turns," Kennedy said to which Murphy smirked.

"Am I correct in assuming none of you are Trust Fund babies?" Adam said. "And can afford to hire a private investigator to follow her around so we don't have to? No? *Damn.*"

Good news is, she's at the museum most days," Kennedy said. "So, we've only got to watch her early mornings and evenings when she gets off. She's got to eventually lead us somewhere, right? Like The Tomb?" I mean, what does every secret society hold in common?"

I shrugged.

Redrum smiled. "Clandestine gatherings."

# DOTTY

The next day after school, I opened my laptop in my room. Although I was supposed to be doing homework, I pulled up my browser and typed "Illuminati" into the search engine.

Unprepared for the deluge of information, speculation, and unclear ties to other organizations such as Freemasonry, Knights Templar, and Assassins to modern secret societies like the Council on Foreign Relations (CFR), Trilateral Commission, and Bohemian Club, I had no idea what I'd gotten myself into.

The more I read, the more the information pulled me in, and although a lot had been recorded about the origins, ideals, dates, and names of founders and members of these groups, there wasn't much else except big glaring question marks. What were the members of these 'sacred orders' doing? And why were so many of the world's most powerful and influential people listed among their membership?

A light knock on my door snapped me out of my studious trance, and Mom peeked her head in. "Ciman?"

I leaned back in my chair, balancing it on two legs. "Yeah Mom, what's up?"

She grinned, glanced behind her, and opened the door fully. "You have a visitor."

I dropped back onto all four legs of my chair. "Redr—!"

"Dotty!" She looked up at my mom with an awkward chuckle. Mom looked confused, like I didn't even know the name of the cute girl visiting me at home.

"Dotty," I said. "How's it going?"

"Good. Thought we could study together." Even though she wasn't carrying a backpack.

"Yeah, sure."

Mom nodded as Dotty entered, hovered for a minute, beaming as though she were about to send us off to prom, then finally took off down the hallway, leaving my door half ajar. She was probably happy I'd made a new friend so soon after the move.

I looked over at Dotty, who was busy taking in the movie and sports posters plastering my walls, the books on my bookshelf, the dirty clothes scattered across the floor, my hand-me-down furniture, brightly colored pillows and bedsheets, stickers, and everything else.

Again, I leaned back on my chair. "It's kinda messy. Sorry."

"Don't be sorry," she said, still nosing around. "I came unexpected. You can learn a lot about a person from their underwear. She stopped at a few framed photos of me with my parents and two younger siblings on my bedside nightstand.

"I like your family," she said. "Your mom's nice."

"Thanks. Yeah, she is."

"You doing homework?" Dotty asked, turning to face me.

I immediately closed my laptop.

She grinned. "Or looking at porn?"

"No, I'm not looking at porn." I hesitantly re-opened the laptop to show her the screen, and she walked over, squinting for a better look.

"You're doing *research*." She put a hand on my shoulder and leaned in, her hair tickling my ear.

"Learning anything interesting?"

I nodded. "Yeah, sure, lots of stuff."

"*Scary* stuff?" She looked at me, our noses almost touching, and I leaned back a bit.

"Meh."

"Raises a lot of questions, doesn't it?"

My brow furrowed. "Uh, yeah. Sort of."

She stood upright with a quick spin, and her hand left my shoulder. She flopped backwards onto my bed, sighing up at the ceiling. "Can be pretty unnerving, the thought of powerful, unsavory people constantly trying to take over the world."

"What do you mean?" I asked. She had an uncanny way of piquing my interest. Like talking about my underwear.

"Yeah," she said, sitting up and propping herself on one elbow to face me again. "Think about it. History teaches time and again that whenever a population is conquered or too heavily controlled, they revolt for the simple fact that people want to be free. But what if the powers that be could socially engineer us to have nothing and be happy about it, to be slaves, yet be okay with it? Then they could conquer the world once and for all."

"What?" I laughed. "Like a Bond villain? Or Pinky and The Brain, trying to take over the world? By the way, should I call you Dotty? Or Redrum?"

She smiled. "Redrum in the club. Here? Dotty."

I returned the smile.

"Things have changed in the world," she said. "Look around. Powerful people have always been trying to dominate the globe—even from the beginning. *However . . .*" She swung her legs around to sit upright on the side of the bed in front of me. ". . . Now they have *new* tools: A.I., bots, cameras, phones, media, drugs, quote/unquote vaccines. Government control, media conditioning, social engineering, NSA, FBI, CIA, blah, blah, blah. It's tiresome thinking of all the ways they try to watch and influence us. Even our food!"

My chair came down again. "Guess I never thought of it that way. Makes sense, I suppose."

She continued. "I suspect that some powerful set of forces has decided consent of the governed is too dangerous to tolerate. So, it's begun to unhook it. They are, after all, the enlightened ones, the *illuminated* ones, and we poor and middleclass, we're just . . . *cattle.*"

I had only ever kissed one other girl—actually *she* kissed *me*. But in this moment, I wanted to kiss Dotty. *Odd*, considering our topic of conversation.

Maybe she could sense it too, which is why she jumped to her feet to continue making a sweep of my room. *"Anyway . . ."*

I turned back to face my computer.

"What did you mean by the *'quote/unquote'* vaccine?" I asked, changing the subject."

"Well, 'vaccines' today are not vaccines," she said in her singsong tone. Not by definition. They are gene transfection technology. Haven't you heard of all the mothers that had a bunch of regular pregnancies pre-Covid, then a bunch of miscarriages immediately following?"

"That's not what all the leaders have been telling us," I said.

". . . Yeah," Dotty said, "Same people that told us that Jeffrey Epstein killed himself. Hey, do you want to go get some ice cream?"

I stood up. "Yeah, let me go ask my mom."

"Cool." She pushed through the door. "I also want to head over to Kennedy's and see how the surveillance is going. I better call him first."

"You didn't call *me*."

"You're not Kennedy . . . And I didn't have your number."

"But you had my address. And—*I'm not Kennedy*—what's that supposed to mean?"

"I looked it up—took two seconds. Give me your phone," she said.

"Pushy," I replied.

"Get used to it." She quickly put her number in my phone and called herself. "There. Now I have it."

"Mom?" I asked, finding her downstairs folding laundry.

"Yes," she said. "You can go. But be home by 8:30."

"Can we make it 9:00?"

"Fine."

"Sure thing. Thanks, Mom."

And we ran out the door. Actually, Dotty skipped.

# GARBAGE

Chomping down the last of our waffle cones, we swung by Gabe's house on our way to Kennedy's. Apparently, everyone else was busy.

"Can't believe you didn't wait for me to get ice cream," he said, disgruntled.

Since our mouths were full, he decided to do the talking, and, in true form, started with a joke: "So, a Mormon walks into a bar. The atheist bartender says, Did you hear about the guy that got his LSD and LDS mixed up? Instead of going on a trip he went on a two-year mission. Oh, and what the hell are you doing in my bar?!"

Dotty giggled, but I had no idea what he was talking about.

"Nothing?" Gabe said. "Oh, come on! I even came up with that one myself."

"I got it," said Dotty. "*Kinda* funny. Good job."

When we arrived at Kennedy's place, his little sister greeted us at the door and pointed us down the stairs. To our surprise, Murphy was there too, helping Kennedy hook up his laptop to the TV.

"Murphy? What gives?" Redrum threw up her arms. "We texted you."

"You did?" Murphy straightened and checked his phone. "Oh. Sorry. Yeah, I can hang out." With the crack of a smile, he leaned back down to fumble with the HDMI cable.

"What are you doing?" I asked.

A video feed of the Peabody Museum entryway suddenly popped on screen, and Gabe perked up. "You didn't."

Kennedy beamed. "We did."

"How many?" Gabe asked.

"Three." Murphy pulled up a video surveillance app on his phone also connected to the feed showing the entry, the Egyptian wing of the museum, and right outside the door to Ahlgren's upstairs office. "We ordered three of these tiny cameras online—they're awesome. Practically undetectable. I'll forward you all the link so you can help us monitor. And they weren't cheap, so you guys can pay us back later."

"Wait, what?" I asked.

The screens suddenly went dark, and Murphy cursed, re-checking his hard connections, and sitting at his laptop to try and bring them back up.

"He lives like he types," Kennedy said, breathing over his shoulder. "Fast. And with a lot of mistakes. But he's a good guy."

"Shut up," Murphy muttered, intent on his prompts.

The idea of surveillance sounded cool, but after a moment's thought, I wasn't too keen on the idea of staring at videos of random people perusing a museum at all times of the day. "Who's going to be watching this?"

"We don't have to," Murphy said, "'cause we also got . . . *these.*" He held up a tiny device about the size of a nickel between his thumb and pointer finger.

"Is that a GPS tracker? How'd you afford it?"

"I sold my Dad's Star Wars poster—he'll never miss it."

My impression of the group continued to gain credibility.

Kennedy patted me on the shoulder. "Very good, Ciman. Yes, and you're welcome, we've already placed them."

"Placed them?" Redrum said, *"Where? On whom?"*

"Where else?" Kennedy asked. "On Ahlgren's person. Er, her purse, rather. Her *very* expensive purse."

"How?" I asked.

"When she was about to ask me on a date," he said, shooting me a wink. "By the way, Murphy, when you said you followed her to The Tomb, did you actually see her go inside?"

"No," he answered. "She entered a neighboring building."

"I thought so."

"Why?" I asked. "Why is that important?"

Kennedy grinned. "Because no one ever enters or exits The Tomb anymore . . . at least, not through the front door."

"What," I said. "So, The Tomb's abandoned?"

"No," Murphy said, "I'm sure it's still in use."

Redrum lit up. "By way of underground passage."

An interesting thought. "So, what, we're watching for Ahlgren to return to the surrounding buildings again? To what purpose? To see who she associates with? How often she goes there? What will that tell us?"

"Patterns can be *quite* telling," Murphy said.

"And . . ." Kennedy said, disappearing into his room and returning hefting two large white garbage bags. We sift through these." He opened the bags and dumped their contents all over the floor. "And don't worry . . . there's more."

"Garbage?" I asked. "Is that . . .?"

Redrum stepped forward, way too excited about the prospect before us. "Ahlgren's trash."

"You've got to be kidding me," I said. "You stole her trash? Does *she* have cameras?"

"I was careful," Kennedy said defensively.

Kennedy, Murphy, Gabe, and Redrum knelt and began sifting through the rubbish—which was remarkably clean for garbage straight out of the bin.

I sighed, and reluctantly joined them on the floor. "Apparently, I had no idea what I had gotten myself into when I took the oath."

"Just wait," Kennedy said. "By the way, Murphy, any news on the sarcophagus?"

Murphy shrugged. "I emailed the pics to my uncle's friend, and he said he'd take a look when he found some time."

"Cool, thanks man."

"Mm-hm."

At first, I had no idea how serious everyone was about this stuff, but I was beginning to understand. I just hoped Ahlgren wouldn't find the tracker, cameras, or learn that someone was stealing the refuse out of her garbage bins at home.

I wanted to ask the question, but I didn't want to hear the answer. "Is all this . . . *legal?*"

Murphy shook his head. *"Technically—"*

"Like any reporting journalist or whistleblower worth their salt, we live and operate in the gray area," Kennedy said. "However, garbage is *not* private. Otherwise, NSA, FBI, and CIA would be breaking the law every day."

Still, that 'gray area' comment made me uncomfortable.

An hour later, after sorting paper, plastic, and responsibly isolated organics, the torn-up or shredded pieces of several financial and other documents surfaced.

I drew a long breath and sighed, focusing on the shredded white pieces, while Redrum plucked out a fine, sparkly, beige-colored cardstock. "What do you think *that* is?" I asked her.

She dug through the piled paper shreds to find similar artifacts, and we all began helping her locate and re-assemble the pieces. After another 15 minutes, it began to come together into a somewhat recognizable format.

Thick, expensive paper. Fine cursive type in a foreign language. Matching stationery. And luxury—if cryptically symbolic—stylistic logos of feathered masquerade masks and triangular watermarked patterns in gold.

"What is it?" Redrum asked. "A trifold brochure?

"Not just a brochure . . ." Kennedy said, carefully taping it together and studying it more closely, ". . . It's an *invite*."

"Invite to what?" I asked.

"Obviously some black-tie affair," Kennedy said.

"Is it obvious?" Gabe asked. "I mean, what language is that? *German in Hebrew characters?*"

"Think we could get our own invites?" Kennedy asked, ignoring Gabe's comment. "Or maybe we don't need any—that looks like an address. Who's got a tux?" He glanced over at Redrum. "Or an evening gown? Anyone?"

# MRS. ORWELL

I couldn't focus in any of my classes. Math, science, Spanish, reading—*Who cares?* Dotty's explanation of the corruption of world powers kept banging around inside my head, and health class proved no different. Did Kennedy really intend on crashing a mysterious black-tie affair in the middle of the Connecticut woods on Sunday night?

Mrs. Orwell finished up a PowerPoint about the human body's digestive track and accessory organs, and immediately sprung a pop quiz on all of us to see if we'd been listening. I hadn't, so I struggled through the questions up until the bell rang.

I glanced back at Adam, who sat in the back corner of the classroom, but as usual, he ignored me. I had also come to realize Mason's sister, Rosi, was in my class, but I wasn't sure she even knew I was in the club (that she rarely attended). She too, ignored my glances.

"All right," Mrs. Orwell said, looking up from her desk at the students. "Go ahead and turn in your papers before you leave for the long weekend. If you're not finished, I suggest you finish quickly." She flashed a sweet smile, but it didn't change the fact I wanted to crumple up my pop quiz and shove it down her throat.

Adam, Rosi, and most of the other students packed their bags and turned in their papers, leaving only myself and a handful of other students to sweat the last few questions, and stress making the buses before getting left behind.

Completely guessing on my last few answers, I jumped to my feet, and tossed my paper in the bin at the corner of Mrs. Orwell's desk. As I made to run out the door, Mrs. Orwell grabbed me by the arm, stopping me.

"Ciman," she said.

I froze. "Yeah?"

"I understand you've joined the school's Conspiracy Club, is that right?"

"Uh, yeah. Is that okay?"

"Of course. What a great group of kids, huh?"

I raised my eyebrows with an awkward nod. "Mm-hm. Yep."

"So . . ." she said, tapping her violet-painted fingernails over her desk, "How do you like it? What do you think?"

"It's . . . *something.*"

"Have you learned anything . . . *interesting?*"

My mind bounced from disturbing initiation practices to the agendas of evil cabals and world powers, to slavery, death, and secret meetings. "Um, you know, the usual stuff."

"Uh-huh." She tilted her head to one side as though putting me through my own personal lie-detector test. "Well, I'm glad you're a part of the group. I've been worried about them not having enough members to qualify as an official school club, considering the last few dropouts."

"Is that why Kennedy asked me to join?" I asked.

"No, no," she said, standing from her chair. "No. I'm sure that has nothing to do with it. Don't you go getting me in trouble. I just wanted to say *Welcome.* But may I ask, what drew you in? What interests you about secret societies and the mystery school teachings?"

"Um, I don't know," I said. "*Friends* . . . I guess."

"Ah," she said. "Of course. Herd animals."

"Excuse me?"

She laughed and rested her hands on her narrow hips. "We humans are such herd animals, aren't we? So easily driven to protection and companionship."

That seemed an odd thing to say to a student. All I could think of was Dotty's comment about cows. In fact, this whole conversation felt awkward, and the beaming look on Mrs. Orwell's face didn't help.

"You know, from the vague reports I've been getting from the group lately, I'd say you're all up to something."

"Better than being down to nothing," I replied.

"Maybe," she said with a hint of playful skepticism. "Well, Ciman, I'm sure you'll bring great insights to the club." Again, that unnaturally white grin.

I pointed at the door as the last few students turned in their quizzes and ran to their lockers, leaving me alone with the teacher. "I uh—I better go, or I'll miss the bus."

"Yes," she said, gesturing her permission to leave. "Go. Have a great weekend. And stay out of trouble . . . *And get your friends to stay out of trouble!*"

"Will do," I said, bowing out of the room. "Thanks, Mrs. Orwell!"

# THE EVENT

Crammed into the back of Adam's gray sedan not made to carry so many passengers, my face was basically smashed against the rear passenger-side window. Redrum sat on Kennedy's lap in the front passenger's seat—which I wasn't so keen on, but they had been friends a long time before I ever showed up. Adam's crazy driving swung us recklessly off the Pearl Harbor Memorial Bridge, onto a link road, through the suburbs, and on to the country.

The moon hung high; its ghostly glow muted through a thick fog. Proceeding down a dark, tree-lined road, no one talked, likely all of us dwelling on similar anxieties as the ones churning in my thoughts. Staring out the window at the deep blue sky peeking here and there from behind the black silhouettes of trees, I wondered if this was truly our best idea. I was almost certain that when we arrived at the party, we would take one look at the gated-off entrance, the high-brow attendees, and the lurking guards, and immediately leave to return home. After all, this was the very definition of 'in over our heads'.

"This is *spooky*," Redrum said, breaking the long silence, to which everyone simply nodded.

At length, we passed the entry gates of a large country house that appeared through the trees to the right, where two men in dark coats waited as sentries. Right as Kennedy's phone beeped and said, "You have arrived," a sign showed the name of the house as "Westbury."

"Did you see that?" Kennedy exclaimed. "Those guards?!"

Adam let off the gas, and the car slowed. "Shall I—?"

The two men stepped forward and watched the car closely.

"No, no," Kennedy said. "Keep going! We obviously can't go in through the front."

"Right." Adam floored it again, and we took off.

"Where should I park?" Adam said.

"Find a turn-off that's kind of hidden."

"Trees are pretty thick," Adam protested.

"How about up there?" Redrum said. "Is that someone else's driveway?"

"No, I don't think so," Kennedy said. "That should do."

Adam pulled off the road behind some low-hanging branches and shut off the car.

"We sure about this?" said Murphy, like a gangly puppy with his tail tucked between his legs. "We're going to stand out like sore thumbs in a room full of adults."

"I can't disagree with him," Gabe said. "If they get one look at us, we're screwed."

"That's why we have masks," Kennedy said. "It is a masquerade ball. We'll scope it out, and if everything looks kosher, we'll find a way in."

Redrum took Murphy and Gabe's side of the argument: "Says the one among us that looks most like a grown-up."

"Come on, guys," Kennedy smiled. "Where's your sense of adventure?"

I gulped, as mine seemed to slide down my throat.

"Ciman's ready," Kennedy said, slapping me on the shoulder. "I can see it in his dead eyes. You all look stunning in your penguin suits."

It was Redrum that looked breathtaking in her gown, but of course I could never say that out loud.

The Conspiracy Club crept stealthily through the thick underbrush of the forest, careful to try and keep from getting snagged on branches or messed up in the leaves and grass. For this to work, we couldn't show up at the door looking like we'd stumbled in from day camp.

We could see the lights growing through the trees, and mysterious music playing at a distance. Cold moonlight, chirping crickets, and the far-off hoot of an owl raised my goosebumps. The glimmering sheen of limousines and some of the finest and most expensive vehicles I had ever laid eyes on parked around a vast entry drive next to the extravagant manor came into view.

"Dear me," Kennedy said. "Look at this place."

As we approached the perimeter of high-end stone and metal fencing, we looked around for any guards or hidden surveillance cameras as well as a way over, and we took our time.

"Looks clear," said Murphy.

Kennedy nodded and led the way, climbing up an overhanging tree, and, one-by-one, we hopped the fence behind some well-trimmed shrubbery.

Slinking around the side of the sprawling property, we zeroed in on a crowd of party guests arriving in their suits and evening gowns. Some donned black hooded cloaks and all wore full-faced Venetian carnival-style masks of every conceivable design and color.

"This is our chance," Kennedy said. "Quick. Put on your masks."

We did as we were told and followed Kennedy to the rear of the entering procession.

I couldn't count the number of limousines lined up each side of the driveway of the vast country house set amidst its own grounds. Other vehicles I could only dream of affording were also ferried up the drive by valets and parked around the back. People in glittering dresses and suits of the finest materials stepped out and walked up to the main doors, held open for us by masked doormen. Barely audible were the whispers of lined up guests as they entered one at a time, and they all repeated the same obscure Germanic phrase: "die göttliche Frau." When we arrived at the door, my heart beating out of my chest, we too were greeted by the finely dressed gentlemen. "Good evening," one of them said to Kennedy.

"Evening," Kennedy replied, obviously deepening his voice, and extending his posture. "The password is: 'die göttliche Frau'." He spoke louder and more succinctly than those before him, likely so we could all hear the phrase more clearly.

"Thank you, sir," said the doorman, gesturing with white gloves for him to enter, which he did.

Then, we all followed his lead, carrying ourselves with as much 'adultness' as we could muster, and made our way past the threshold.

Once we had all entered, Redrum slowly and elegantly stepped back and took my arm. We walked a wide pillared hallway behind the other guests and were approached by a masked butler who wore a hooded cloak. The sound of strange music rose in the background.

The butler too greeted each of us in turn asking for the password, which we gave, then thanked us as another stepped up behind him to ask for our jackets. We all kept them.

"This is strange," I whispered to Kennedy, who also fell back next to Redrum and I."

I could only imagine the freaked-out expressions on the faces of Mason, Gabe, Adam, and Murphy under their masks—probably a lot like mine.

"Shh," Kennedy said.

"The password," Redrum whispered. "What does it mean?"

"'*The divine woman*'," he answered. "It's German. Heard the other guests in front of me."

We walked toward another door, which another masked man opened for us. We entered, perfectly content to follow the crowd. As we came in through the anteroom door and walked slowly across the space, a steward, also masked, elegantly gestured us through heavy velvet drapes into a vast hall, its balconies, columns, and walls all finely carved in marble. The crowded hall quickly filled with people dressed similarly, and everyone began to quietly converse. High above us, aerial dancers in skin-tight uniforms slid down long red silks, and athletically maneuvered into elegantly pleasing poses across the ornate ceiling.

"Wow," I whispered. "Spared no expense."

A spotlight suddenly lit up a single kneeling figure in the center of the room. The house lights dimmed, along with a series of electric candelabras. This must have been the only person on the entire premises not wearing a mask. Sweat beaded on his forehead. Another figure wearing a crimson cloak stepped forward from the crowd waving an incense burner in one hand and holding an aureate staff in the other. An alter built of human skeletons raised from the floor like something from a Vegas magic show. In the faint lamplight, what appeared to be corpses draped in shrouds also lowered from the ceiling, but they moved, silently writhing amongst the aerial dancers.

At the far end of the hall, a blindfolded quartet dressed in white changed their strange tune to something slower and deeper. The eerie music resonated through the hall and up to the marble balconies and galleries where even more cloaked and masked spectators hushed and moved to watch the ceremony.

"This is an initiation," I whispered to Redrum.

She nodded ever so slightly.

The crimson-cloaked man shuffled around the lone figure and then moved behind him. He bowed deeply and the kneeling man prostrated himself on the floor before the alter. Two acolytes in purple robes approached from either side, and took the man by each arm, turning and dragging him over the alter, face up. One of them tied a pink ribbon smeared with blood on his forehead and hung a crucifix and an amulet around the man's neck. The other removed the man's outer cloak as five shrouded figures approached, blood-stained and mumbling incoherently. They threw themselves down in supplication as if in prayer. Sudden light bathed the scene as a funeral pyre was lit.

I watched wide-eyed as they tossed the man's cloak into the fire. As the pyre blazed higher, a large form rose from the inferno.

The booming voice of a priestly initiator spoke out, low but distinctly and with great authority. Finding it difficult to determine its source, the initiate found himself repeating the words of the oath. *"In the name of the Enlightened One, I swear to sever all bonds which unite me with mother, brothers, sisters, wife, relatives, friends, mistress, kings, superiors, benefactors, or any other man to whom I have promised faith, service, or obedience. I name the place in which I was born. Henceforth, I live in another dimension which I will not reach until I have renounced the evil globe which has been cursed by Heaven. From now onwards, I shall reveal to my new chief all that I have heard or found out, and I shall also seek out and observe things which might otherwise have escaped me. I honor the Aqua Tofana, the poison, the quick and essential medium of removing from the Earth through death those who oppose truth and those who try to take it from our hands. I shall avoid the temptation to betray what I have now heard. Lightning will not strike as rapidly as the dagger which will reach me wherever I may be should I betray my initiation."*

A seven-branch candelabra bearing seven black candles was set before the candidate along with a bowl containing what looked like blood. The candidate washed himself in it, and even drank a small quantity, before being escorted away.

From a column furthest away from the spectacle we watched as the crimson-cloaked man banged his staff on the carpet to officially end the opening of the ceremony and command the figures and everyone else to their own business of conversing and merry-making.

While my friends and I tried to fathom what just happened, two figures glided down a marble staircase, and took a more than passing interest in us.

"C'mon guys. Let's go to another room." Kennedy moved off, and we tentatively followed.

The figures on the stairs continued to watch us as we left. One of them, a man, wore a Venetian plague mask, while the other, a woman, hid behind a beautiful mask with feathered plumes. There was a sinister air to them both.

The Conspiracy Club members moved down a red-carpeted corridor which, like the hall, had walls of carved marble. Large mirrors on the walls reflected our small and out-of-our-depth procession.

"We don't belong here," said Redrum. "We should leave. Now."

I nodded in agreement.

"Where's Murphy?" Gabe asked, and we all stopped to look around for our gangly friend.

"Murphy's Law must have bit him in the ass," Adam said, to which we shook our heads.

We were all there together and accounted for except Murphy, who was nowhere to be seen.

At the end of the long corridor, right off the main hall where we had witnessed the initiation, the two figures from the stairs followed us.

"What do we do?" I asked.

"I feel like we're in danger the longer we stay," Redrum said, clenching my arm tighter than before.

"Keep moving," Kennedy said. "Murphy's got to be around here somewhere. Search the house. We'll find him, and we'll leave."

An obese man in an over-sized hat and mask, suddenly appeared and grumbled something inaudible, shuffling past us with a masked young woman at each arm.

Many doors and archways ahead led off in several different directions to rooms full of people, and our group took pause to try and guess which one we should take.

"Should we split up?" Gabe asked.

"No," Kennedy said. "We have to stay together."

Another woman moved past us and eyed Kennedy seductively through her mask.

I turned back once again to see the ominous couple closing the gap between us. "I don't like this."

We entered a room with a long central table, searching for Murphy to no avail, and continued through the house, attracting several strange looks from those gathered as we went.

We searched the anteroom and library with its oak-paneled walls and bookcases full of leather-bound volumes. Still, no sign of Murphy.

The couple from the stairs cornered our group by the roaring fire under the mantle.

"Have you been enjoying yourselves?" asked the woman.

"We've had an interesting look around," Kennedy said.

"May I ask," said the man in the Venetian plague mask, "For clarification. Where did you receive your passwords for the house?"

"Our passwords?" Kennedy said, calm and collected. "With our invitations."

A ballsy gamble, considering the invitation we pieced together from Ahlgren's garbage contained no such key word.

Two additional masked figures walked up behind the couple and interrupted the conversation. "If you could please come with us," one of them said, "I'm afraid there's been a misunderstanding involving your friend."

"What misunderstanding?" I asked. "Who are you talking about?"

"Please," said the other man, casually motioning for us to follow them out of the library. "This way. If you'll come with us, we'll get everything sorted out."

We sheepishly followed the two men, and the couple closed in behind us.

"You know, we've been going over the guest list," said one of the men, "and the numbers are simply not adding up."

I glanced back at the woman walking behind us and noticed her violet fingernails hanging at her sides. No way in Hell could that be Mrs. Orwell. I simply couldn't tell from her voice.

She put an arm over my shoulder as the man put a hand around

Redrum's back. They both stared down at us through the small black eye holes of their respective masks.

"So, children uninvited," said the woman. "Seems you've been . . . naughty. This party has an age requirement."

"Where's our friend?" I asked, thinking myself courageous. Gabe, Mason, Adam, Redrum, and Kennedy looked at me and shook their heads.

"Who is your friend?" asked the woman.

"He's skinny. Tall. Has red hair."

"My boy, lots of our guests have red hair. I'm afraid you will need to be more specific. We wouldn't want an unfortunate mishap to befall your friend, which can often happen to poor little birds who wander uninvited where they ought not."

The cold glare from behind her flower-crested mask picked me apart from the inside out.

I gulped back the bile in my throat. "Something tells me you already know his name . . . and ours.

"My sweet dear, we know a great many things."

"Will you let us go?" I asked.

"Will you promise never to reveal what you have seen in this house this night?"

I gulped again. "I promise."

"And what about your friends?"

"We promise," they all said in unison.

"If you do, you will receive the direst of consequences . . . *And* your families."

The butler received us at the front door and opened it. "You may go."

"What about our friend?" Kennedy asked.

"You may go," the masked butler said again.

"Be careful," said the woman, "And keep your mouths shut. We'll be watching you."

We stepped outside, and the heavy door closed behind us.

# KEN ALLEN

Adrenaline pumping, we hopped the wall, climbed down the tree, and tore through the dark woods with dizzying abandon. Our suits and Redrum's gown whipping through grass and past tearing branches, all I could hear were our frantic footfalls and my own heavy breathing. This was the last thing I expected to be doing when I joined the Conspiracy Club.

When my lungs were about to explode, we finally broke free of the forest, and made it to the open, moonlit roadway, then back to Adam's car, where we had left it.

We gathered around, catching our collective breath, bewildered at what went down.

"Did that really happen?" I huffed, ripping off my mask before everyone else.

"I can't believe it," Adam grinned, staring down at the road. "We're *Ken Allen.*"

"What?" I asked.

*"Ken Allen,"* Adam repeated through labored breaths. "C'mon, the *orangutan?"*

"You've lost me."

"It's the most infamous animal escape in modern history. Ken was the resident orangutan at San Diego Zoo. Known for his repeated breakouts from enclosures thought to be impossible to escape."

"Have you all forgotten about Murph?!" Redrum shouted.

"Keep it down," Kennedy said, which drew a wide-eyed glare from Redrum which I hoped would never be aimed at me. I couldn't, however, help but admire her sweaty, disheveled look in that elegant nightgown gone *Survivor*.

"They still have him back there!" she said with utter desperation.

"So what do we do about it?" Gabe asked. "We obviously can't go back."

"No," Kennedy said, thinking. "We can't. Not now."

"Not ever!" Gabe exclaimed. "You heard that woman."

"I'm glad Rosi sat this one out," Mason said thoughtfully.

"Adam," Kennedy said, leaning back against the car, craning his head skyward, and squeezing his eyes shut. "You're basically a walking encyclopedia . . . There are *two* sides to Illuminati: their odd rituals and their ideals. Am I remembering that right?"

"Yes," Adam said. "And I'd say that ritual back there was pretty damn odd."

"Agreed." Kennedy swallowed. "Murphy, Murphy, Murphy. What else? What are we missing?"

Adam opened the driver's side door and sat behind the steering wheel. Mason and Gabe jumped in the backseat, likely the most eager to leave. I joined them as we waited for Kennedy and Redrum to sit down.

Kennedy thought out loud. "They've always used symbols like the owl, adopted pseudonyms to avoid identification. Do you think that was actually Illuminati? Or some off-shoot or sex cult pretending?"

"I didn't see any owl symbols in the house," said Mason.

"Me neither." Redrum plopped down in the front passenger seat, deflated.

"I don't know," Adam said. "The original order had complicated hierarchies like Novice, Minerval, and Illuminated Minerval that divided the ranks—Their different colored robes could have something to do with that."

"True." Kennedy squeezed in under Redrum and shut the door.

Adam started the car and pulled back onto the highway.

I let out a sigh of relief. The car didn't blow up.

"In the beginning," Adam said, "Illuminati members didn't trust anyone over 30, because they were too set in their ways."

"Pretty sure I saw some 'Floridas' in there," Gabe said, "Despite their masks."

"Yeah, me too," Adam said. "Other reports of rituals are harder to confirm, but we know members were paranoid, thus the spy-like protocols to keep identities secret."

"Like kidnapping red-headed high school kids?" Redrum exclaimed.

"What could Murphy have done that they would single him out?" Mason asked. "Or did he just wander off like he does sometimes?"

I had an idea and thought I'd add my two cents. "The cameras and bugs following Gabe's 'Propaganda Minister' at the Peabody Museum—weren't those purchased in Murphy's name?"

"Technically yes." Kennedy lightly banged his forehead on the side window. "I feel responsible."

"We're *all* responsible," I said.

"No," Redrum corrected me. "Actually, only the masked bastards back there are responsible."

"I still can't figure it out," Adam said. "Most think the Illuminati were only mildly successful—at best—in becoming influential."

From what I had read online, they also promoted a worldview that reflected Enlightenment ideals like rational thought and self-rule, which I guess could have loosely applied to those masked crazies at the party. Anti-clerical and anti-royal, the Illuminati were closer to revolutionaries than world rulers since they sought to infiltrate and upset powerful institutions like the monarchy. Did the Illuminati ever manage to control the world? Jury was still out, and with no assurances it would ever return.

"Of course," Adam went on, "those like us who are open to the idea they may have successfully taken over and still control the world today—I mean, look, if an all-powerful group does dominate, we probably wouldn't even know about it. Those people back there? I'm with you, Kennedy. They probably are some off-shoot or sex cult doing their own messed-up things."

"I never said that's what I thought," Kennedy said.

"Well, whether you did or didn't," said Redrum. "Step on it and get us the hell out of these woods. We'll look for Murphy when it's light out. Those creeps give me the creeps."

# THE MISSING GINGER

Stepping off the bus two days later, exhausted for lack of sleep, I joined Redrum, Kennedy, Adam, Gabe, and Mason in front of the high school. Two cop cars parked next to the buses drew my attention, the whole place abuzz with conversations about our friend, the missing ginger.

Redrum looked particularly gloomy.

We met up and walked solemnly toward the front steps with the others.

"Any word on Murphy?" I asked quietly.

"I went back and searched the woods around the house the next morning," Kennedy said. "Only a few hours after we had left."

"Let me guess," Adam said. "You didn't find anything."

Kennedy shook his head.

"Maybe we should go look again after school," said Redrum.

"He's not there," Kennedy said. "I swear. I looked everywhere. They had to have taken him somewhere—"

"Or worse," Adam interjected. "To those people, secrecy is everything. The end justifies the means if you know what I mean."

Kennedy stopped halfway up the stairs and glared at Adam. "Your nickname for the club should have been *"Ass,"* you know, after the Assassins."

"I'm just sayin—"

"I know what you're saying," Kennedy retorted. "Until we hear an official police report or see a body, I'm going to assume our friend is still alive. And we are going to do everything we can to find him."

"We could tell the police," Redrum said.

"You heard the threats," said Gabe. "If we talk, we're all dead, and our families."

"Maybe they were bluffing." Redrum shrugged.

Gabe balked at her. "And you're willing to take that risk? They don't seem like the type of people to make hollow threats."

*"An unfortunate mishap,"* I whispered.

"What's that?" Mason said.

I thought back on the night Murphy was taken. "Did you hear what that woman in the feather mask called it? She called his kidnapping an unfortunate mishap."

"Yeah," Mason said, "so . . .?"

*"Mishap* suggests a kind of failure, a *mistake.* We were never supposed to be there. They even asked us flat out where we acquired the password for the house."

"So, what are you saying?" Kennedy asked.

"Surely they'll take him somewhere to question him," I said.

"Or they've *already* questioned him and discarded the body," said Adam.

At that, Kennedy punched the school doors open violently, and everyone stopped to look. "Again . . ." turning to face Adam. ". . . *Ass.*"

Adam glared back, rolled his eyes, and took off for class.

After the tension dropped, Redrum piped up. "Let's meet again after school. Usual place?"

We all nodded and headed for our lockers, the furtive and not-so-furtive stares of fellow students boring into us as we went. Apparently, most everyone was aware of the missing kid's membership in the Conspiracy Club.

# HEALTH CLASS

In health class, I found it particularly difficult to focus. Flanked by Adam in one corner, and Mason's sister, Rosi, in the other, with Mrs. Orwell up front, Murphy's disappearance screamed at me from all sides. Although Rosi had never talked to me before, apparently Mason had given her my name.

"Psst, Ciman," she whispered. "Ciman, Mason told me everything. What do you think happened to Murph?"

I shook my head to one side with a slight shrug, avoiding eye contact. Now wasn't the time.

Mrs. Orwell, halfway through a presentation about the body's digestive system, glanced my way, but all I could see were her fingernails—no longer violet, but a glossy light green.

I carefully listened to her voice as she explained the three primary processes of mixing food, moving it through the digestive tract, and using chemicals to break it down into smaller molecules. I tried to remember the tone of the woman in the mask and compared to Mrs. Orwell's, yet I couldn't tell if they were the same woman.

When the bell rang, and everyone grabbed their stuff to hurry out the door, I confronted Mrs. Orwell at her desk.

"Ciman!" she said with a smile, "You know, I've been wanting to talk to you. How was your long weekend?"

"Do you know where Murphy is?" I blurted.

Her face went sullen. "Well, I—That's actually what I was going to ask you. Isn't it terrible? I mean, when his parents reported him missing, the administrators, we—D-did *you* . . . see him this last weekend? Did you meet with the club over the break?"

I shook my head, but she could probably tell I was lying, woman from the party or not.

"Did you paint your fingernails?" I asked.

She lifted her hand, splaying her manicured fingers proudly. "Why yes, I had them done over the weekend. How did you—?"

"Weren't they purple before? Last Friday?"

She tilted her head. "Uh—why do you ask?"

"*Were* they purple, like a *violet* color before?" I repeated.

"Uh, yes, I suppose—surprised you noticed—"

"Where did they take him?"

Her brow furrowed. "Where did ... *WHO* ... take him? I'm confused."

I let out a sigh. "So am I."

"I feel like there's something you're not telling me, Ciman." Mrs. Orwell leaned forward in her chair, and I stepped back against a desk on the front row.

I re-secured my backpack straps over my shoulders. "Join the club."

As I turned to leave, Mrs. Orwell stopped me. "Uh, Ciman."

"Yes, Mrs. Orwell?"

"If you do hear anything about Murphy, please let me know."

I swallowed the lump in my throat, nodded, and left her classroom, more confused than when I had entered.

# DEAD PRESIDENTS

As I approached the backstage area, I found Adam and Kennedy arguing behind the curtains. "Freemasonry boasts six million members," Kennedy was saying, "many of its past grand masters residing in the upper echelons of world governance. Don't tell me their influence can't be felt by all."

"That's not what I'm saying," said Adam. "I agree with you. My point is it's not *them*. Look at the history—Both founding fathers, George Washington, and Thomas Jefferson, revealed their awareness of the Illuminati in their letters, that it was a melting pot for the various cults, sects, and societies, all of which claimed secrets passed down from ancient sky gods. But—."

"Yeah, yeah," Kennedy said, "Members combining arcane wisdom with modern scientific knowledge for enlightenment. But that's all a bunch of bullshit. There was more to it—greed, a-a search for power. The unpublished—"

"It's not—" Adam threw up his arms as I walked up between them. "Yes, apart from Illuminati structure and doctrines, there could have been some of that, but just because it started in Germany—"

"Exactly!" Kennedy said. "Yes. Germany. Remember the letter? The invite to Ms. Ahlgren? What was it written in? *GERMAN!*"

"What does that have to do with Murphy?" Adam asked.

"Oh, I don't know, maybe his whereabouts," Kennedy said sardonically. "In danger of speaking rhetorically," I said, "Am I ...*interrupting*...something?"

Fuming, they both took a backward step, obviously at an impasse.

"So, I still haven't figured out if that feather-masked woman was Mrs. Orwell or not," I said. "If it was, she most certainly has an ulterior motive;

she obviously knows who we are and what we're doing. Or . . . she's daft."

"And her fingernails?" Kennedy asked.

I looked down at the carpet with a long exhale. "No longer violet."

"That's great," Kennedy said. "And you could be misremembering it."

"No," I said. "She confirmed they were violet."

Redrum and Gabe joined us on the stage, with Mason straggling behind. And then, surprisingly, Rosi walked in.

"Any news?" Gabe asked.

"No," Kennedy snapped.

"Nothing actionable," Adam added, a little more gently.

"What about the surveillance?" I asked. "Ms. Ahlgren? Surely, she was at the country house."

"How would we know that?" Kennedy asked, clearly agitated. "According to the trackers, she's only been at home, the museum, and running errands on campus. Besides, she threw away her invite, and none of us saw her at the party."

"How could we have?" Redrum asked. "Everyone was in a mask."

"You can still kinda tell," Kennedy said.

With a tone laced in sarcasm, Redrum replied, "Oh, *okay.*"

"Look," I said. "We're all upset about Murphy but taking it out on each other won't solve anything."

"Hi Rosi," said Adam, with a shy glance.

"Hey guys," she replied. "My apologies for playing the absentee member. With Murph gone, I feel kinda bad about it. What happened?"

Mason bumped her shoulder. "I told you what happened."

"Well maybe I wanna hear it from *their* perspective."

"We snuck into what we think might have been an Illuminati initiation ceremony," Gabe said. "Murphy disappeared. We searched the house, got made, and . . . they kicked us out."

"And this was on Sunday night?" Rosi asked.

We all gave a slight nod, and everyone went quiet.

"Did you recognize anyone?" Rosi glanced around at each of us.

"No," said Adam. "Everyone had masks."

"Ciman noticed a woman's violet fingernails," Mason said. "Remember? And they matched—"

"Mrs. Orwell's." Rosi finished the thought and looked at me. "I noticed them too."

I tried not to blush and turned to Redrum, who said, "Enough about the fingernails."

"I agree," I said.

"So what do we do now?" Rosi asked.

Another few seconds passed in silence.

"Wait," said Mason. "According to the U.S. Census Bureau, the city has a total area of 20.1 square miles, of which 18.7 is land and 1.4 is water."

"Yeah," said Kennedy. "So . . ."

"Never mind," Mason huffed, "I lost my train of thought."

Everyone rolled their eyes.

"Hang on," I said. "Kennedy, you mentioned the trackers we put on Ms. Ahlgren had her running errands on campus. You mean Yale's campus, right?"

"What other campus would I be referring to?"

"Has she been in the building next to The Tomb since Sunday?"

Kennedy turned to Gabe who pulled out his phone and opened the tracker app. "Quite a lot, actually."

"Wait," Rosi said. "You think Murph might be there? You're not actually going to try and get inside The Tomb."

"It's a thought," Kennedy said.

"Well I'm out." Rosi folded her arms. "I've heard too many stories."

"Afraid I'm out too, fellas," Mason said, following his sister's lead. "I can't do a repeat of the other night—I'll have an anxiety attack."

"I'm not coming either," Adam said, walking over and standing by Rosi. He glanced at Kennedy. "You can't even agree with me that Frankfurt was the birthplace of both the Illuminati and the Rothschild empire."

"Perhaps it's good for you two to keep your distance," I said.

"Well now I feel bad." Rosi folded her arms. "I didn't mean to break up the club."

"I'll go," I said.

"Me too," said Redrum.

"I guess I'm on the fence," said Gabe.

Redrum put an arm around him and pulled him in. "Nope. You're coming."

"I guess I'm coming," he said.

"All right then," said Kennedy. "Let's go to The Tomb."

# ON CAMPUS

As the four of us parked and walked across the Yale campus, an awful, sickly feeling began to rise and swirl in my gut, yet I couldn't help but think of my grandpa's words: "If you find yourself getting too comfortable in life, you're doing something wrong." Gabe and Redrum seemed in good spirits, considering. Kennedy too had lightened since we left Adam at the school. However, I think it bummed him out that Rosi and the rest didn't want to come along, not even as backup.

"I think maybe we need a code word or phrase," Redrum said. "You know, if things go terribly wrong."

"How about *'Cracker want a Polly'?*" Gabe suggested.

"That's a terrible code; sounds like a black guy talking about a white guy who wants a stripper."

I couldn't help but grin.

"Forget the code," Kennedy said. "This is why conspiracy theorists are laughed at. Our friend was literally kidnapped by people wearing masks."

"Hey, speaking of kidnapping," Gabe said, "I have a new joke: Did you hear about the Catholic kids that wandered into the basement of a Washington, D.C. pizza shop?"

"No," I said. "Tell me."

"Well, they heard a lot of things, but they did not hear the *Sound of Freedom.*"

"Too soon," Redrum said.

"Is it?" Gabe said.

Kennedy looked disgusted and handled something inside his jacket pocket. Part of me hoped it was a recorder the FBI was listening in on.

"Remember back when some believed vaccines carried microchips to track us?" Redrum said. "I just wanted to point to the phones in their pockets."

"Or that 'the rona' was dumped into the water supply?" Gabe added. "If someone truly believed the world's entire water system had been poisoned with snake venom, one would think they'd attempt to filter their tap water before drinking it."

"Good point." She noticed Kennedy's worrisome level of focus and said, "This is a good plan, Kennedy."

"I know."

"You know? Well, okay then."

"You're smart, and I believe in you," she said with a teasing tone.

"Yes, I am. And of course you do," Kennedy replied.

Puzzled, I spoke up. "W-what is happening?"

"I'm stroking Kennedy's ego, because he is an egomaniac, and I believe with enough positive affirmation, and with our help, he can pull this off."

"*Egomaniac.* That's a bit excessive," Gabe said. "*Braggart* maybe. No, that's too close to narcissist, and Kennedy's too nice a guy for a label like—"

"Okay, fine," said Kennedy. "I'm either a talented genius, or I suffer from delusions of grandeur. Either way, I keep things interesting. Will everyone shut up now?"

We walked in front of a dark, windowless building framed by two stone pillars, an old stone sepulcher.

"*The Tomb,*" Redrum muttered with an almost reverence.

We all took a few moments, giving the eeriness of the building enough time to settle into our spines. Then we continued around the corner.

Redrum pointed at a nearby white stone building that took up most of the adjoining block. "That the one Ms. Ahlgren entered this morning, and never exited?"

Gabe looked down at the map pin on his phone and nodded. "Yeah. This is it."

The four of us waited outside the massive university building for someone to show. After about twenty-five minutes, a fair-haired young man that looked the part of a rich Yale fraternity boy approached the main steps. Kennedy quickly walked up next to him and grabbed him firmly by the arm, stopping him.

"Hey!"

*"Skull and Bones,"* Kennedy said, staring him in the face. "Do you accept?"

The young man's eyebrows loosened like he'd been made by the uninitiated, and Kennedy knocked him out cold.

"Yes," Redrum said, jokingly. "I accept."

"Not a word to anyone," Kennedy joked back, throwing one of the young man's arms around his shoulder, and gesturing for me and Gabe to come over and help him, which we did.

# THE TOMB

When the young man awoke, gagged, and secured to a chair with duct tape in a dark, non-descript room, he began to groan and struggle against his restraints.

"Finally," said Kennedy. "For a while there, we were afraid you wouldn't come back."

He moaned at us angrily, but his muffled words were indecipherable.

"Let me help you with that." Kennedy carefully unwrapped the duct tape from his head and neck, which yanked at the poor kid's skin. He spit out the gag and glared at Kennedy with demonic eyes. "Get me the hell out of here or you're all going to burn."

"We will let you out," Kennedy said. "But we have a few quick questions first."

"I've taken an oath of secrecy."

"We're aware," said Redrum. "We just want you to get us inside The Tomb."

"Impossible," the young man scoffed. "You have to be chosen."

"And, no doubt, they have your worst secrets," Redrum said. "Still, you're going to show us in."

"No girls allowed," he said.

Redrum tilted her head to one side. "Who's to say anymore? And didn't Ms. Ahlgren go there this morning?"

That drew some surprise out of him, but then his face went a shade of fearful. He shook his head. "I want no part of this . . . whatever *this* is."

"We're trying to get our friend back—" I said, but Kennedy raised an arm, shutting me up.

The young man looked over at me, then at Redrum, Gabe, and Kennedy. "What is this? Are you even college students?"

"What's your name?" Kennedy asked.

"I'm not going to tell you my name—"

"It's James," Kennedy said. "Or do you prefer 'Jim'?" He held up the kid's sorted-through wallet in front of him.

"Who's your girlfriend?" Kennedy asked, holding up a picture of a pretty brown-haired thing from the photo gallery on his phone. "You know, you should really password protect—"

*"Go to Hell."*

"I'm gonna try not to." Kennedy drew a deep breath, and looked over at me, making me feel even more uncomfortable than the already unsettling situation—which I didn't think was possible. "Don't worry," Kennedy said to the young man, "We won't ask you who the 'Master of Secrets and Orders' is."

"That's an outdated reference," said the kid.

"If you say so. How do we get inside?"

"You don't," he said. "I already told you. It's impossible."

Kennedy walked over and forcefully untied him from the chair, ripping viciously at the duct tape until it all came off. The young man stood, knocking the chair over, and with angry fists moved to attack Kennedy, but a cocked handgun pointed at his forehead stopped him short.

I gasped, not knowing beforehand Kennedy had brought a gun. "Kennedy—"

"Shut up." With a stiff arm, Kennedy motioned for the young man to follow us out of the building, and back to where we had started.

"What was all that for if you're just going to let me go?" asked the hostage.

"We needed you to know we're serious," Kennedy said.

With the gun now pressed against the small of James's back, Kennedy pushed him up the steps toward the main doors. Redrum, Gabe, and I acted as shields to passersby so they couldn't see Kennedy and 'Jim's' awkward embrace.

We entered the building, and James took us to an elevator bank halfway down the central hallway. Apparently, the pulled gun supplanted the kid's commitment to secrecy. Pressing three of the buttons on the bottom row simultaneously, the elevator took us at least three floors below basement level.

When the doors opened, it became clear we had either entered The Tomb or its modern-day equivalent. A darkly lit stone sub-basement with heraldic flags and mystical Teutonic symbols dating from the fourteenth century, the age of the original Bavarian Illuminati, draped over the walls, drew us out slowly.

"Where is everyone?" Kennedy pushed James forward with the stalky silver barrel of the handgun. "No red-hooded intitiates? Upperclass Bonesmen? No candles or black ceremonial robes?"

"I don't know," he said. "And it's not like we meet every damn day."

"Right. Of course. But then, we found you coming into the building, didn't we?"

"Is this where you became one of the 'best and brightest'?" Redrum asked James, to which he said nothing.

"A little cooler than the place *I* was initiated," I said. "If I'm being honest."

She threw a quick smirk my way.

We heard the echoing footsteps of high heels, and a woman emerged from a dark passageway far below the high balcony level that ringed the room.

Ms. Ahlgren. "What is this?" she said. "Who are—? Oh yes. I remember. From the museum. And . . . *James?*"

"I'm sorry, Ms. Ahlgren," James said, sounding genuine. "They have a gun."

"No, they don't," she said. "They're high school kids."

Looking squarely at Kennedy, she said, "Shoot me."

Kennedy kept the weapon at James's back.

*"Shoot me, dammit!"* she said more sternly.

Hand shaking, Kennedy raised the handgun at her and fired. The bullet hit her in the chest and bounced off.

She didn't even flinch.

"It's an airsoft gun, you idiot," she said to James with a cold glare. "Leave! Go! Bring the others."

Like a kitten learning to walk, James scampered out of the dark hall.

"People like you will never understand people like us," said Ms.

Ahlgren. "You're just kids. Why would you do something so stupid?" She pulled out her purse and rummaged around inside.

We all glanced at one another at a loss.

She pulled out the trackers and cameras and threw them in our faces. "We don't want to kill you—You're only children! But you leave us no choice."

"By 'us' do you mean Jay Z and Kanye West?" Redrum said to try and break the tension.

It didn't work. This woman was a 'Karen'.

"What is this place?" Kennedy asked.

"You already know," said Ms. Ahlgren. "I mean, hell, you've even been through my trash. I have never met anyone that has tried so hard to bring down the wrath of the most powerful people in the world."

"Most Americans today don't actually believe in the Illuminati," said Kennedy.

"And neither should you," she answered. "Oh that the world were so simple. You should stop telling yourself lies—You might start believing them."

"Only if you promise to practice what you preach."

"Even after all this, you're still determined to make an adversary of me. Do you deem that wise?"

"She makes a fair point," I said.

"Are you students of Weishaupt, and still don't grasp the meaning? Enlightenment requires nothing but freedom. Freedom to make public use of one's reason in all matters. Now I hear the cry from all sides. "Do not argue," the officer says. "Only drill." The tax collector: "Do not argue, pay." The pastor: "Do not argue, believe." Only one ruler in the world says: "Argue as much as you please but obey." We find restrictions on freedom everywhere. But which restriction is harmful to enlightenment? Which restriction is innocent? And which advances enlightenment? I reply, the public use of one's reason must be always free, and this alone can bring enlightenment to mankind."

"Voir dire," Kennedy said.

"What?" I asked.

"It's French," said Redrum. "Means: To speak the truth."

"Conspiracy theorists aren't 'conspiracy theorists' when the theories prove real," said Kennedy.

"They are when said proof is kept from the masses," Ms. Ahlgren replied. "Have you not learned that public perception is everything? You've been inculcated with idealism and rationalism. You have become free thinkers, have you not? You're not so unlike the original members. A fraternity of progressive, even radical thinkers, who could change the old conventions of their world."

"That's a fine speech," said Kennedy. "I'm curious. How long did it take you to memorize it?"

"You snot-nosed brat." She let out a chuckle, her head bobbing with such hubris, such smugness. "We only take advantage of people's desperate need for order."

Kennedy smiled. "Or maybe the order's best kept secret is that it holds no secrets of any significance, and you poor assholes just refuse to feel unimportant."

"That's funny coming from a kid who's only been alive eighteen years and doesn't know a damn thing. In fact, I bet you have never seen anything like . . . *this* . . ."

A few awkward moments passed, and we glanced at one another uneasily as she stood there holding her purse.

Kennedy scoffed. "Never seen anything like wh—?"

The woman screamed as a hurricane wind burst from the blackness behind her. The sudden force flung the purse from her hand, and it hit the wall. With outstretched arms, she lifted off the ground like a demon possessed. A chorus of moaning voices arose from beneath and around us and echoed off the high ceiling.

We all fell backward, reeling.

The woman's pupils rolled back in her head and the whites of her eyes took over. Hovering high above, it was as though she struggled to slowly look down upon us.

Gabe passed out and collapsed backward onto the stony floor.

"I knew she was a witch!" cried Redrum.

*Or Propaganda Minister, as Gabe would say if he were still conscious.*

Scooting back across the stone flooring, we all huddled together as the wind and clamor continued to beat against us.

At length, the woman descended. Her shoes finally touched the floor, and her head slumped forward, eyes closed. The wind ultimately ceased, and all went quiet.

Behind Ms. Ahlgren, a gathering of young men in black robes emerged and surrounded us. They carried someone into the space and dropped them on the floor in front of us.

We flinched before recognizing the limp figure as Murphy—His fiery red hair was unmistakable. He looked pale, unconscious, and like he'd been roughed up and bloodied.

"Murphy!" I shouted, rushing to his side. "Murph, are you alright?"

He didn't move at first, but then he moaned and strained to open his bruise-blackened eyes. "What'd they do to you, Murph?"

Ms. Ahlgren drew in a long breath and raised her head. "An unfortunate mishap," she said.

*If they meant to kill us, now would be the time. We knew too much.*

I dragged Murphy back to Redrum, Kennedy, and Gabe, and we all crouched together under the shadowy gaze of at least two dozen Bonesmen, and the museum curator turned legion.

"Whatever takes place here is never to be repeated," said the woman.

The Bonesmen restated the phrase like a mantra with their many voices echoing throughout the sepulcher.

They all stared at us and waited.

"Whatever takes place here is never to be repeated," I said.

"And your friends," said Ms. Alghren.

They too uttered the words.

*But we're not Bonesmen,* I thought.

Only now did I notice Ms. Alghren's violet fingernails.

"Do you promise?" she said.

"Yes, ma'am," I said.

"All of you!"

"Yes, ma'am," We spoke almost in unison.

"Get them out," said Ms. Alghren.

The black-robed Bonesmen assailed us, and tore us from one another, dragging us away through the dark, struggling, kicking, punching, scratching.

Hefting us forcefully off the stone floor, at least four or five to one, we were no match for the horde of black. It was like being dragged off the field by the football team from Hell. They took us through winding passages, and I lost sight of Murphy, but I could hear Redrum screaming. Blinding flashes of light passed over our faces as we struggled, but I soon found the more I wrestled them, the more I got beat or yanked around, so I relaxed.

The darkness persisted, but I could sense an upward winding staircase. Kennedy's shouts and Redrum's cries kept me oriented. I heard an electronic pin pad, and the sound of metal locking mechanisms disengaging. A heavy door swung open into the blinding light of a streetlamp, and I was pushed outside, tumbling violently onto Gabe and Murphy. Kennedy and Redrum landed on top of us, and we all rolled across the grass.

The heavy door with no outer handle, knob, or keypad closed behind us with a thud.

We all groaned in pain and writhed on the ground.

I crawled over to Redrum first. "You okay? Redrum?"

"Call me Dotty. You know, I'm almost flattered—never have so many guys tried to cop a feel in such a short time."

"Dotty." We helped each other onto our knees and approached Murphy and Gabe, who were both recovering consciousness.

"Murph?" I said, "Gabe? You guys gonna be all right?"

Gabe gave off a shallow groan.

Murphy strained to roll over. "Put me in a car," he said, "and get me out of this place."

Kennedy made it to his feet first and lifted Murphy off the ground with one arm. "I must admit, I'm a little surprised we're all still breathing. I guess this batch of Bonesmen haven't been trained as assassins."

"That comes later," Gabe said, clutching the back of his head "You know, after they become politicians. Oof, my head."

"You took a pretty hard fall," I said.

"Yeah," he replied, "but Murph got it worse."

"I'll be all okay," said Murphy.

I turned to Kennedy. "You really laid it on back there. Why do you think she let us go? And what was that whole possession thing? Was it, like, some kind of Satanic display?"

"Or she's the female version of David Copperfield, and only trying to scare us."

"If that was it, I'd say she did a pretty bang-up job," said Gabe.

"What do you mean?" I asked. "You were only awake for half of it!"

He punched me in the already-sore shoulder, and we all started hobbling back toward the car.

Murphy noticed Redrum staring and called her out on it.

She gave him a funny look. "I was just admiring that unruly mop of hair."

# NEVER HAPPENED

*"Whatever takes place here is never to be repeated,"* Redrum said in a mocking tone.

We all laughed as we ate our Friday night ice cream. Reunited with Adam, Mason, Rosi, and—most especially—Murphy, who was healing nicely from his wounds. When the doctors, hospital nurses, or even law enforcement asked him who perpetrated the physical abuse, he simply told them, "Some kidnapper," and that he never got a good look at the man's face since it was always covered.

"Don't know how you can keep it all a secret," Kennedy said to Murphy as he stirred his Oreo shake.

"Same way you are," he replied. "I value life."

"Off topic," I said. "Do any of you ever feel like you're being followed? Or watched?"

"Why?" Rosi asked. "Have you seen someone following you?"

"Maybe," I said. "I dunno. It's hard to tell. At night, I'll look out my window and see shadows, figures maybe—It's probably nothing, my imagination. Nevermind."

"No. Sometimes at school I see kids I don't know following me around," Redrum said. "But you're right. It's probably just some dorks too afraid to ask me to the dance."

"On another note," I said, hugging Redrum close, "Murphy, we're dying to find out about the sarcophagus from the Peabody Museum. Did your uncle's friend ever get back to you with an analysis of your etching?"

Murphy smiled. "Yeah, he did—He was actually pretty excited about it. He said the hieroglyphics from the etching dealt mostly with Thoth, the Egyptian god of writing, magic, wisdom, and the moon. Apparently, he was one of the most important gods of ancient Egypt alternately said to be self-created or born of the seed of Horus from the forehead of Set. In other words, Thoth is the Egyptian god of . . . wait for it . . . *enlightenment.*"

"Huh," Kennedy mused. "Enlightenment. Suppose it makes sense Alghren would have something like Thoth plastered all over her office wall . . . *I still can't get that image out of my head.*"

"What image?" Rosi asked, pausing from her ice cream with a confused look.

Kennedy glanced up at her from his shake. "The image of her hitting on me in the Peobody lobby."

We all chuckled, but less so among the four of us who there in The Tomb that night.

"On a side note," Adam said, "I think a bunch of those people from the party have left town."

"Oh yeah?" I said.

"Yeah, including Kennedy's favorite museum curator. She's even left the museum. They've all up and disappeared. Our trackers and cameras were likely found and destroyed—it's all gone dark on Murphy's app."

"That's true," Gabe said.

"I still don't know why you won't tell us what happened at Yale," Mason said.

"Other than finding Murph by a tree in front of The Tomb," Redrum said, "Nothing did happen."

"Do you think we embarrassed them somehow?" Gabe asked the group, diverting the subject.

"I don't know," Kennedy said, "But at that country house, there's a 'For Sale' sign out front with no evidence anyone ever lived there."

"Never happened," I said. "Right?"

Kennedy shot a knowing glance back at us. "*What* never happened?"

———

In a survey of conspiracy theories recently conducted, zero people claimed that groups like Freemasons, Skull & Bones, or Illuminati control politics or world government. Even so, the Illuminati persist in our collective consciousness, serving as the butt of jokes and the source of lizard people rumors.

However . . . would you bet your life on it? Or your family's lives?

## THE END

# About the Author

Brian C Hailes has written/illustrated over 60 titles, including four illustrated novels, Hotel California, Avila, Defender of Llyans, and Blink, two graphic novels, Devil's Triangle, and Dragon's Gait, and many short stories and children's books. He also illustrated several Girl of the Year books for American Girl, and Continuum (Arcana Comics). In 2002, he won the L. Ron Hubbard Illustrators of the Future award and is now an official judge for the contest. His artwork has been featured in the 2017-2024 editions of Infected By Art. He currently lives in Salt Lake City with his wife and four boys, where he continues to write, draw, paint, and produce videos regularly. His work can be seen at:

HailesArt.com
DrawItWithMe.com
Instagram: drawitwithmeofficial
Facebook: drawitwithme
ArtStation: bchailes

Also Look for These Titles from

# EPIC EDGE PUBLISHING

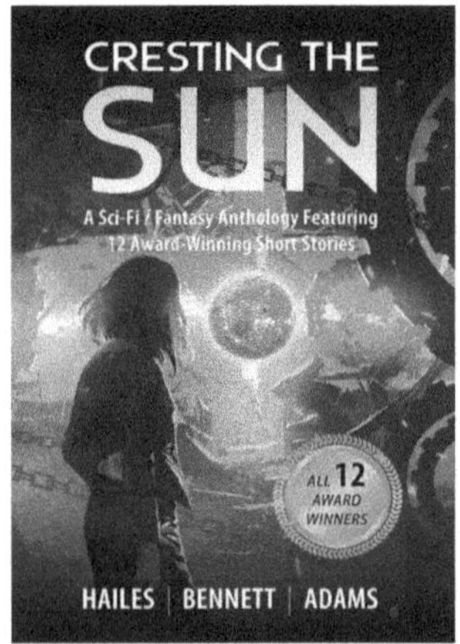


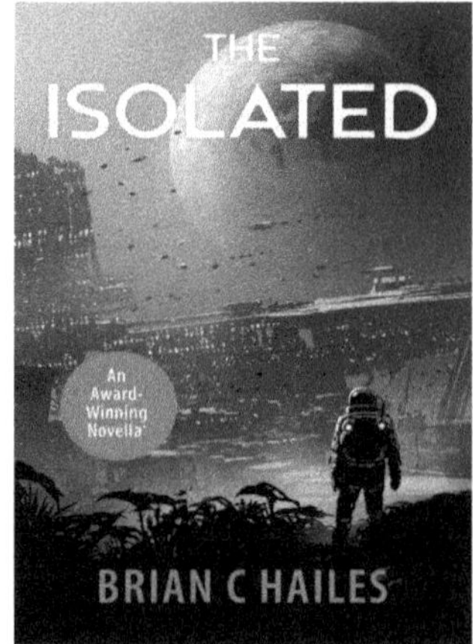

DEVIL'S
TRIANGLE
THE COMPLETE GRAPHIC NOVEL
HAILES          CASSELMAN

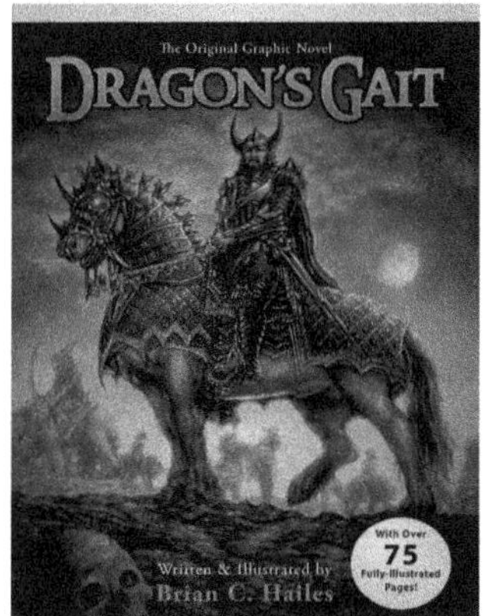
The Original Graphic Novel
DRAGON'S GAIT
Written & Illustrated by
Brian C. Hailes
With Over
75
Fully-Illustrated
Pages!

An Illustrated
Science Fiction
Novel
AVILA
HAILES          DEFENDI
COMING SOON!

DRAW IT WITH ME: THE
DYNAMIC
FEMALE FIGURE
BRIAN C HAILES

DRAW IT WITH ME A
STUDY OF THE
HUMAN FORM
With Over 100 Sketches, Gestures & Artworks
of the Male & Female Figure
BRIAN C HAILES

KAMIKAZI
BRIAN C HAILES          JOHN ENGLISH

DRAW IT WITH ME: THE
ELEGANT
FEMALE FORM
An Intimate Study of the Beautiful Feminine
Figure in Varied Chic & Classical Poses
BRIAN C HAILES

COLOR MY OWN
HALLOWEEN
STORY
AN IMMERSIVE,
CUSTOMIZABLE
COLORING
BOOK
FOR KIDS
(THAT RHYMES!)
by BRIAN C HAILES

DON'T GO NEAR THE
CROCODILE
PONDS
BRIAN C HAILES

IF I WERE A
SPACEMAN
A RHYMING ADVENTURE THROUGH THE COSMOS
BRIAN C HAILES
ILLUSTRATIONS BY TITHI LUADTHONG

HERE, THERE BE
MONSTERS
A RHYMING QUEST TO FIND TERRORS OF LEGEND & MYTH
BRIAN C HAILES
ILLUSTRATIONS BY TITHI LUADTHONG

Can We Be Friends?
STORY BY EDIE NEW
ART BY CINDY HAILES

# ILLUMI-NAUGHTY

## A Conspiracy Club's Unfortunate Mishap

As newcomer to New Haven High School, Ciman (with a "C") and his plucky group of Conspiracy Club member friends, take on the task of uncovering the workings, influence, and hidden power of the world's most secret order. As they sort through the bizarre riddles surrounding The Illuminati, they are stunned to discover a trail of clues hidden within the fabric of society, including Skull and Bones, Knights Templar, assassins, whistle blower accounts, and the local, on-campus museum—clues visible for all to see and yet ingeniously disguised by the pernicious cabal.

Even more startling, the museum curator, deeply involved in the secret society, has been guarding a breathtaking secret concerning the whole of the human population. Unless Ciman and the gang can decipher the maze-like puzzle—while avoiding the faceless adversary who shadows their every move—the explosive truth could be lost forever.

---

*"Hailes delivers yet again with this pulse-pounding (and hilarious) adventure. His eccentric and well-written teens take on the oh-so-nefarious men (and women) behind the proverbial curtain, and the outcome is utter enjoyment!"*
—*A.M. Rothschild*

*"A delightful masterpiece . . . Some of the most fun I've had with any book—all the twists, turns, and quips! There are much by way of conspiracy references, but delivered with a laugh and therefore worth exploring. A literal page turner in my humble opinion.*
—*J.P. Rockefeller*

FICTION | SCIENCE FICTION | ACTION & ADVENTURE

www.ingramcontent.com/pod-product-compliance
Lightning Source LLC
Chambersburg PA
CBHW040841010826
48978CB00012BB/845